The Children's Lottery

by

E.R.Reilly

PUBLISHED IN GREAT BRITAIN BY
SANTIAGO PRESS
PO BOX 8808
BIRMINGHAM
B30 2LR

Email for orders and enquiries:
santiago@reilly19.freeserve.co.uk

ISBN 0-9539229-9-5

Printed and bound in India by Authentic India, Secunderabad - 500 055,
email: publisher@ombooks.org www.ombooks.org

Mum was sitting on the toilet reading the paper. Suddenly, she jumped up and started screaming and shouting. It sounded as though a big hairy spider had frightened the life out of her. But she had not seen a spider. She had seen something in the paper that had alarmed her. It was my lottery number! Mum and Dad don't believe in gambling, so they never buy a lottery ticket of their own. When the Children's Lottery came out, I thought it would be fun to get one.

Mum jumped up and started running about the house. She jumped up so quickly that she never even got dressed properly. She had tucked her dress into her knickers and she looked really silly.

She was shouting, "Josh has won the lottery! Josh has won the lottery!" She was jumping off the floor with both feet together and then she ran around in small circles. She looked as though she was doing a rain dance. In fact, she looked as though she were a person who was being worked by remote

control and who was doing a rain dance. She jumped up and down again and she hit the lightshade with her head and it went flying.

Dad asked her if she was sure and she said, "Yes! Yes! His number's in the paper. Josh has won the lottery! Josh has won the lottery! Ahhhhhhhhhhhhhhh!"

And then Dad started jumping up and down with her. To be honest, I was really happy, but I wasn't happy because I'd won the lottery, I was happy because Mum and Dad were so happy. I had never seen them so happy. It's not that they were usually sad, because they're not, but I've never seen them jump up and down for joy before.

I don't know why I bought the lottery ticket in the first place because I never really believed that I would ever win it. Mum says that lottery tickets are for people who have not got enough imagination to think of something to spend their money on. She didn't stop me from buying a ticket, though.

My Dad hates the lottery. He says that

the millions of pounds being spent on lottery tickets could be put to far better use helping people who really needed the things that money could buy. But he lets me make up my own mind about things. He didn't stop me buying a ticket either. I bought it with my birthday money.

My Mum was phoning everybody we knew. She was still dancing around the house and screaming half an hour after she read my number in the paper.

Dad said, "Sit down, for heaven's sake. You'll do yourself a mischief in your condition."

Mum tried to sit down, but she sprang straight back up again. She was just too excited to do anything but jump around and scream, and that was all there was to it.

I've never seen my Mum like that before. She is normally a happy person, but not so happy that she can't stop herself jumping up and down.

We had lots of visitors that night. Some

people who came to see us had never been to our house before. I can tell you this for certain: having a winning lottery ticket makes you very popular indeed.

Nobody would normally have described me as being popular. I suppose people would probably think of our family as being a bit odd. My Dad runs a charity. It's called "People Need Pals". Mostly, people refer to it as PNP. The charity is for people who need a bit of help in their day-to-day lives. Sometimes people are not very good at reading, so they find it quite hard to sort out their bills. Sometimes they need a bit of help finding work or sorting out their benefits. Dad's charity also works with people who have Alzheimer's. It's really sad when people get Alzheimer's because they become confused and can forget things. They can even forget the names of people that they know really well. They can even forget who their family are.

There have been times when my Dad hasn't come home at all because he has spent all night looking after someone who was upset about something.

I love my Dad. I wouldn't change him for any Dad in the world.

My Mum is really nice as well. She works in the OXFAM shop. People give their old clothes to her and she washes them and takes them into the shop and sells them. The money that she makes goes to OXFAM. They are a charity like Dad's, but Dad's is a very small charity and only looks after local people, and OXFAM is one of the biggest charities in the world.

They look after people all over the world. If people in places like Africa cannot find clean drinking water, or if they haven't got the right tools to look after themselves, then OXFAM will help them. All of our clothes come from the charity shop, to be honest. It's never bothered me. In fact, I really like it. From time to time, my Mum will collect up a load of my clothes and put them in black bags and take them off to her shop. A few days

later, she'll come home with a bag full of new clothes. I love opening up a bag full of new clothes and trying them on.

Ours is a big old house with lots of rooms, and, in the downstairs back room, there's a big mirror on wheels in the corner that you can move around. I might find a corduroy jacket with a red cap and a new pair of jeans, or I might find a striped shirt with a pair of flowery shorts. I love it.

When I was a little kid, nobody bothered about it, but since I've been in the Juniors, some kids tease me. I get into a few fights, to be honest. My Mum and Dad say that I should ignore people who say cruel things, but I just can't stop myself. Anyway, I'm not trying to say that fighting is right, because I know it's not, but, if people know that you're not afraid to fight, then they are a lot less likely to call you names.

I'm quite quiet at school. I suppose I'm about average at football. I'm quite good in goal. My best subject is English. I love reading. You know the way I told you that my Mum comes home with a bag of clothes for me? Well, she sometimes comes home with a bag of old books. I love it when she does that. She always does it on my birthday, but she sometimes does it as a surprise when I am least expecting it. It's my favourite time of the whole year when she does that. I like playing football and I like going swimming and watching TV, but, apart from that, I love reading books more than anything else. I'll tell you all about my favourite books and my favourite authors, but first I'll tell you what happened when my Mum found out about my winning lottery ticket.

Mum and Dad said that I didn't have to go to school the next day. To be honest, that was as rare as having the winning lottery ticket. I can't remember one single day when they told me I could have a day off school. Even when I didn't feel well they always said that school was the best place for me.

Mum phoned up the lottery people and

they sent somebody out to see us. I had been using my ticket as a bookmark. Since the number turned up in the paper, my Mum kept the ticket in her hand. She took it to bed with her, but she didn't sleep. Every now and then, she went back to the paper and checked the number again.

When the man from the lottery came, we had finally become quiet. The priest had arrived about half an hour earlier and we were kneeling down in the front room saying the Rosary. We're Catholics and we say the Rosary every Sunday evening. Father Robinson comes to see us every now and then, and we always say the Rosary together. We have beads that help you to keep count of where you are and the prayers we say are called "Our Fathers" and "Hail Marys".

Anyway, we had finished saying our prayers and the house was quiet because you always have to turn the telly off when the priest comes to your house.

When the man from the lottery came,

13

he walked up to the door, but he didn't have to knock on it because Mum was standing there with the door wide open waiting for him. Mum invited him in and asked him if he wanted a cup of tea. When he said he did, Mum told Dad to go and make it. The man said that he had to check the number before he could answer any of our questions. He took a pair of glasses out of his top pocket and he compared the numbers in the paper to the numbers on my ticket. Mum sat on the edge of her seat and followed his eyes. I don't know why, though. She had checked it herself about a thousand million times. When the man said that the numbers matched, Mum started jumping up and down again.

I had one burning question which I was dying to ask him. I bet you can guess what question it was, can't you? Dad brought in the tea and the man said, "Well, now. I'm guessing that you would like to know how much you've won."

Of course, we all said, "Yes!" straight

away, and then we all burst out laughing. As you might have guessed, that was the question that I was dying to ask anyway.

Then he said something that brought us all down to earth with a bump. He told us that I hadn't won anything. We didn't quite know what to think. I felt numb, to be honest. Mum and Dad said nothing.

But then the man from the lottery quickly put us out of our misery. He explained to us exactly what was going to happen.

I was going to have to go to America, to a place called Cleveland to find out how much I was going to win. He told us that I could end up winning millions and millions of pounds! Phew! We had gone from being happy to sad and to happy again in a matter of seconds.

There had never been a children's lottery before. Children were not allowed to buy normal lottery tickets. I think you have to be sixteen before you can buy a normal lottery ticket. But this lottery wasn't the normal national lottery. It wasn't

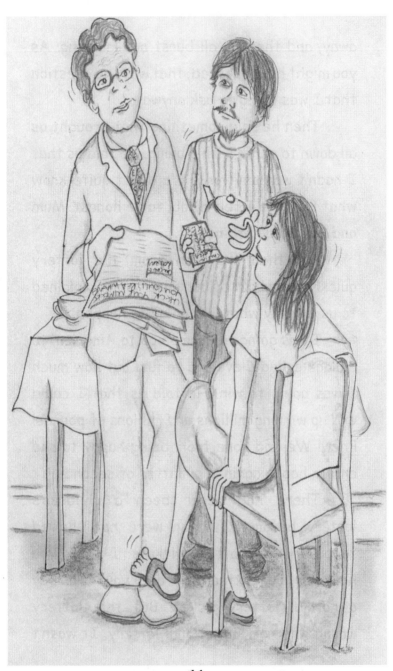

anything to do with the Government. It was an international lottery and it was only for children. An American billionnaire had decided to retire. His computer business was just about the biggest private business in the world. He didn't have any children of his own to leave his great wealth to, so he decided to run a lottery to find someone that he could give his millions of pounds to.

He decided that there would be three winning lottery tickets, but these lottery tickets wouldn't win a certain amount of money. They would win the chance to go to America to be on a reality TV show. The idea was that the performance that each child gave on the TV show would determine how much they would win. I didn't know at the time, but I later found out, that there was to be some gambling on the TV show. I wasn't sure about gambling. That might sound silly because buying a lottery ticket is gambling, but I didn't look at it like that. I just thought of it as being a bit of fun.

So that was that. Before I knew it, I was on an aeroplane and flying off to America. I'll tell you all about the TV show and the other contestants and all of that, but, first of all, I'll tell you how this all left my family.

The first thing that we all had to think about was how we were going to manage all of this. I was in for a very big surprise straight away. My Mum wasn't able to take me to America. I couldn't understand why at first, so my Mum and Dad decided that they had to sit me down and tell me.

It turned out that my Mum was going to have another baby. I was really surprised by this. I had never expected to have a brother or sister. It wasn't something that my parents had ever talked about. It turned out that my Mum and Dad had been told that they would never have another child after me, so they didn't talk about it. My Dad said they had been told that the chances of them having another child were thousands to one, so they just put the idea to the back of their minds and forgot about it. Now that she knew she was going to have another baby, my Mum wouldn't go on an aeroplane because she may have to go and see her doctor at any time.

You are probably thinking that, at this stage, the solution would be simple, and that any normal Dad would just take his son without question. I did tell you that my family is a bit odd. We go to a caravan park for our holidays each year, but we never go for more than three or four days because my Dad always worries about the people that PNP looks after. The trip to America was going to take a month. I knew that this would be a problem for my Dad.

Both my Mum and my Dad told me not to worry. They said that, one way or another, they would make sure that I would get to America and be on TV.

I lay in bed that night for hours, but I couldn't sleep. There were questions whirling round my mind and making my head spin. It would all be a lot easier if I knew how much

I had won. It would be a good deal easier if I knew that somebody was definitely taking me to America, and I wasn't going to wake up and find out that I wasn't going to America at all. I never mentioned this to my Mum and Dad, but I was worried that I wouldn't be allowed to take time off from school. As if all of that wasn't enough for me to be thinking about, I also had to get used to the idea of having a new little brother or sister.

A new little brother or sister! I couldn't get the thought out of my mind. I was already well into the Juniors by the time that I heard this news, so, by the time that my new brother or sister would be old enough to play with, or do anything with really, I would probably be in senior school. It seemed like hours before I finally fell asleep.

Eventually, I did, though, and, in what seemed like no time at all, I was sitting at the kitchen table, having breakfast with my Mum and Dad.

21

----❋❋❋----

My Mum and Dad told me that my Aunty Ann was going to take me to America. I loved hearing that news. Aunty Ann is brilliant.

Whenever she comes to our house, she always brings me a present. Sometimes she brings clothes, sometimes she brings toys and sometimes she brings books. She says that she has never met anyone that has read as many books as me, so she's frightened of bringing me books because she never knows if I have already read them. I never tell her. I just give them to my Mum and she puts them in her charity shop.

Aunty Ann is my Mum's sister. I told you that people might think my Mum is a bit odd. Well, to be really honest, everyone thinks that my Aunty Ann is odd. Mind you, everybody thinks that she's really nice. I've never met anybody that doesn't really like Aunty Ann. If you can imagine someone that usually wears big floppy hats, baggy jumpers and tight skirts, then you can probably imagine my Aunty Ann. She also has a habit of wearing big beads, big earrings and different coloured lipstick. She's going through a phase of wearing orange lipstick at the moment. She's even got some green lipstick. In fact, the green is my favourite.

Aunty Ann knows the words to every song that comes on the radio and she normally sings along with them. When she comes to take my Mum for a night out, she always brings a bottle of wine and they drink it in the kitchen before they go out. They giggle a lot and make up their own dances. They have been doing that since Mum was five and Aunty Ann was three.

Mum and Aunty Ann are massive Robbie Williams' fans. He's a pop singer and they listen to him all the time. When it was my Mum's birthday, Aunty Ann bought tickets for them to go and see him in concert. Me and Aunty Ann in America. I liked the sound of that.

24

I had to go into school to tell all of the children in my class what was happening. Aunty Ann came with me and so did the man from the lottery. School was brilliant about me having time off. As it worked out, I was only going to miss two weeks of school because the half term holiday came in the middle of my stay.

I can tell you this for certain. If you want to go from being the kid that hardly anyone talks to and change into being the most popular kid in the school, then just win the lottery. It's easy. In the playground, people were offering me sweets and biscuits and things. That was strange, wasn't it? I was suddenly going to be rich and everybody wanted to give me things. That doesn't make any sense, does it?

Anyway, everybody wanted to know everything. Every single person in school, including the teachers, wanted to know every single little detail of what had happened to me and what was going to happen to me. I answered all of the questions, and the ones that I couldn't answer, the man from the lottery answered for me.

I began by telling them that I bought the lottery ticket from my birthday money. They asked me who gave me the money to buy the ticket and if I was going to give them lots of money out of my winnings. I explained that quite a few people gave me some birthday money and that I had put it with the money I already had in my savings tin. So, I couldn't really tell who the money was from.

I told them about Mum tucking her dress into her knickers and jumping about the house when she found out that I had the winning ticket. They thought that was funny. The children's lottery was new and there was only ever going to be one, so most people didn't have a clue what it was all about, so I had to explain it all, right from the very beginning.

The children's international lottery was set up by the world's richest man. He is a

multi-billionnaire. He owns lots of different companies. Some of his companies are the biggest in the world and earns over ten million dollars every single day of his life. Now that's rich! His name is Bertie and he is an American. He changed his name, though. He's now called Lord Bertie. His full title is a bit of a joke, I think. He calls himself Lord Stinking-Rich Bertie of Stinking-Rich Mansions. Everybody just calls him Lord Bertie, though.

He dresses like an old fashioned Lord. He wears a top hat and tails and he always uses a monocle. I think he might be a bit funny, too, because he sometimes wears red trainers with his top hat and tails. I thought that I would probably like him. He sounds like somebody from my family, but with lots of money.

Lord Bertie is a kind man because he gives more money to charity than probably anyone else in the world. He supports lots of projects in the world that help people who live in war-torn countries. He also helps people who have HIV or AIDS. Lord Bertie set up the International Children's Lottery because he didn't have any children of his own. His view was that, if he did have children, then they would be very lucky indeed because he was the richest man in the world. He thought it would be fun to find a child from somewhere in the world to make them the luckiest child in the world.

And so, the International Children's Lottery was born. Lord Bertie's plan was to sell tickets all over the world. The tickets were on sale in every continent. There was no limit on how many tickets each child could buy. The only rule was that each child had to buy the ticket themselves, and they had to be fifteen years old or younger. Lord Bertie was allowed to hold his lottery because it was entirely private. All the prize money was from his personal wealth. Every penny of the ticket sales was being given directly to charity. So the children's lottery was very different to the ordinary lottery.

There was also another very big difference. Having a winning ticket did not necessarily mean that you would win lots of money. There were three winning tickets and each ticket enables each child to take part in the children's lottery reality TV show in America. This TV programme would decide who would win the lottery and just how much they would win.

They asked me what the TV programme was going to be like, but I couldn't tell them because nobody had told me yet. I asked the man from the lottery, but he told us that we would find out all about that when we got to America.

In what seemed like no time at all, that's exactly where I was - the United States of America. I had never known anything like it in my life. We travelled first class on the aeroplane. It was absolutely fabulous. We

could have any food and drink that we wanted and Aunty Ann was really funny. She rolled her seat back so that it was like a sun lounger and she put headphones on. She wore her darkest sunglasses and she sang along with all the songs. And, all of the time that she was doing this, she was sipping champagne cocktails and eating olives from a marble dish. Winning the lottery is the best thing in the world because, when you do it, you get to see your family being really happy.

America is a wonderful country. We had stretched Cadillacs to take us everywhere and, whenever it was time for us to get out of the car, the driver opened the door for us. Aunty Ann had a black suit on with a white shirt that had a long collar and she had a little black parasol to protect her from the sun. She was still wearing her sunglasses, so she looked like a film star. She walked into the hotel like a model walking down a catwalk.

When we got up to our room, there was a big jacuzzi that looked out over a balcony and we were on the thirty second floor. The view was the most fabulous view that I had ever imagined in my life. The buildings were all skyscrapers, wide and bright, and the streets were filled with people milling about like those films you see of tiny ants all being busy and purposeful, and then there was me and Aunty Ann just chilling out and taking it all in. I told you that Aunty Ann was a bit mad, didn't I? Well, this will prove it. She picked me up and dropped me into the jacuzzi, even though I had all my clothes on! I could hardly breathe, I was laughing so much.

I started to splash her, but she opened up the big French window and stepped onto the balcony and hid behind the glass. I got out of the jacuzzi to go and soak her, but she pulled the window tight shut and stood there sticking her tongue out at me.

In the morning, a butler wheeled a trolley into our sitting room. There was a feast laid out on it. There was more food than we could possibly eat. There were four different kinds

of sausages. There were lots of different kinds of meat. There were eggs cooked in all different ways. The butler sort of bowed and asked us to ring when we wanted the trolley to be taken away. Aunty Ann asked him what was going to happen to all of the food that we didn't eat. The butler seemed surprised by the question and said, "well, we'll throw it away, of course."

Aunty Ann was livid. She said that she had no intention of all that wasted food being on her conscience, so she told the butler that in future he had to ask us what food we wanted and not to just deliver a whole load of food that was going to end up being thrown in the bin.

She was wearing pink pyjama bottoms and a blue Birmingham City football club shirt, but she didn't bother getting dressed. She put her Doc Marten's boots on and she wheeled the trolley out of our room, down the corridor and into the lift (which they call an elevator). She wheeled the trolley out of

the hotel and stood there giving bacon and sausage sandwiches to passers-by. She is different to most aunties I know, but she's brilliant.

She saved some toast and a big pot of tea and went back to the jacuzzi in our room and lay in the warm, bubbly bath eating jam and toast, drinking tea and laughing out loud about the look on the butler's face.

That night, we had been given an invitation to meet for dinner in the Presidential Suite. We were really looking forward to this because we were at last going to meet Lord Bertie and the other two children.

Dinner was really nice. Lord Bertie's personal staff served dinner and they weren't nearly as stuffy as the hotel staff. Aunty Ann was brilliant again. Before we started eating, she stood up and said Grace. I told you we were Catholics, didn't I? Well, if I didn't, we are Catholics, and Grace is a prayer that we say before we eat a meal. It's just a little prayer to say "thank you" for the food, really.

After the meal, Lord Bertie stood up to talk to us. I liked him straight away. He said that he had heard about Aunty Ann giving food away and he said that he thought it was a good idea. He told us that, in future, only food that had been ordered would be sent to the rooms, even the poshest rooms. I could feel that Aunty Ann was pleased. I think that she liked Lord Bertie as much as I did.

We were introduced to the other two winners. There was a girl from China. Her name was Chu Li and she was only six years old. She could speak some English, but not enough to be able to follow everything that was going on. She had an interpreter who constantly whispered in her ear, telling her everything that was being said. I could see that Chu Li's eyes kept closing. All she wanted to do was go to sleep. Her parents were very different, though. They were wide-eyed and they looked around them like nervous animals

that were trapped in a corner. They gave little bows to everyone and they had big smiles. I liked them.

The third winner was from America. He was older than us. I think he was about fifteen, but he never actually said how old he was. His name was Richard, but everyone called him Richy Rich after the boy in the film. He was really rich already. He wasn't as rich as Lord Bertie, but he was rich enough for his parents to send him everywhere in chauffeur-driven limousines. His Mum stared all of the time. Aunty Ann said that she looked like that because she had had too many facelifts. Her hair was about a foot taller than she was and she had so much make-up on that she looked a bit like a clown. She was wearing so much gold and pearls and jewels, it's a wonder she didn't fall over from all of the extra weight that she was carrying around.

Whenever Richy or his parents wanted a waiter, they snapped their fingers in the air without even looking up. Aunty Ann and

41

I looked at each other when they did that. We didn't like that family at all. I know that you shouldn't make opinions about people like that, but, well, we just didn't like them.

Anyway, we didn't have to like them. We were there to be on a reality TV show. It was my job to try and win the lottery so I suppose that Richy and Chu Li were my opponents, really.

After we had been introduced to each other, and got to know each other a little, Lord Bertie rose to his feet again. The time had arrived, at last we were going to find out what the show was all about.

---- ❋ ❋ ❋ ----

Lord Bertie told us that we needed to listen very carefully because the game that we were playing had now begun. He told us that there were TV cameras watching us now and that anything that we do or say may be put out on TV. He told us that the children's lottery TV programme would be made in three parts and would be shown in every country in which the children's lottery tickets were sold. That was every country in the world. He told us that we could ask the adults with us for advice at any time.

The first thing he told us was that we could stop the show at any time and leave. If we did that, we could leave with one million dollars. He told us that we could rely upon that one rule throughout the three shows. He warned us, though, that we could not rely on anything else. He told us that nothing is what it seems. Everything was part of the game and, if we forgot that, it could cost us a lot of money. He told us that we could have the rest of the evening to talk and think about the news that he had given us. He also told us that he would explain how each show would work out after breakfast tomorrow morning.

Then he dropped something of a

bombshell. He told us that we were not allowed to contact anybody until the end of the final show. This didn't seem very fair to me. Richy and Chu Li had their parents with them, and, although I love my Aunty Ann and she's brilliant, it didn't seem fair that I couldn't talk to my parents. It wouldn't have been so bad if I had been told about it in advance.

I went to Lord Bertie and complained. He tried to tell me that I should be a big boy and that it wouldn't be long before I saw them again. I probably would have just accepted it, but Aunty Ann was having none of it.

She started to stick up for me. She told Lord Bertie that he was a spiteful old man to do such a thing. She told him that it was nothing short of child abuse to take a child half way round the world and then stop him from talking to his parents. Aunty Ann told him that he should be ashamed of himself for being so cruel.

Lord Bertie tried to explain that

this was a game and, if the children could contact people from outside, there could be cheating.

Aunty Ann told him he was a stupid, thoughtless man, if that was the only thing that was causing all of the fuss. She told him that Mum was expecting a baby and that was reason enough for us to be allowed to communicate. She said that the messages that went between us could be checked by the producer of the programme to make sure that nothing is mentioned about the show.

Lord Bertie said that sounded very sensible and he agreed to it.

I think Aunty Ann was taken aback a bit. She was just about to continue ranting at him when she realised that he had given in, and she stopped herself just in time.

Lord Bertie told Aunty Ann that he really liked her. He said that, because he was one of the richest men in the world, everybody was nice and polite to him. He told her that he liked her spirit. I think she liked him too.

Aunty Ann and I went up to our suite and talked about everything that had happened. From that day on, I passed text messages backwards and forwards between myself and my Mum, via the producer. The big thing that Aunty Ann and I had to discuss was the question of the million dollars. If we didn't take the million dollars now, we could end up winning less than a million. But if we carried on with the game, we could end up winning a lot more than a million. We lay on the big white settees in our rooms for a while and, eventually, we decided that it would be best to stay in the game, but, if we ever felt that we might lose the million, we would quickly call a stop and leave with the million.

We had a couple of days to wait for the first programme, so we decided to explore. There was a very nice man called Charlie, who worked for Bertie. He was given the job of looking after us. He had a limousine to drive us anywhere that we wanted to go, and he was authorised to buy us anything that we wanted. Can you imagine the fun we had?

Aunty Ann went shopping. She asked Charlie if she could pick up a few things for presents and Charlie said that he was authorised to pay for anything that we wanted. She bought about five different lipsticks for herself, and then she bought a posh shirt for my Dad. I told her that he would never wear it, but she bought it anyway. She said that it was time he learnt to live a little. She bought a picture of Robbie Williams for my Mum. He's her favourite pop star. She asked Charlie how much she was allowed to spend, but Charlie just laughed and said that it wouldn't make any difference to Bertie. He told us that, in the time we had been in that shop, Bertie had earned more money than most people would earn in their entire lives. So, Aunty Ann walked back over to the make-up counter and picked up another handful of colourful lipsticks.

We went to the pictures. We sat and watched the film with a large bucket of popcorn. We went to a waterworld during the next day. We had a great time - the slides seemed about half a mile long! Aunty Ann asked Charlie to join us, but he said that he had no swimming trunks. Aunty Ann told him to go and buy some. You could tell that he wasn't very keen, but Aunty Ann is one of those people who like to get their own way. She reminded him that Bertie had told him to do whatever we wanted him to do. And this is what we wanted him to do. So, he did it. And even though he was reluctant, he was glad that he did it, because he came in, splashed around and slid down the slides. Charlie enjoyed himself as much as we did.

On our last night before the first programme, Charlie brought us to a great place to eat. It was called Wendy's. I suppose it was a bit like McDonalds or Burger King, but we don't have them at home. We preferred it to the hotel. You see, the hotel was very nice, but it was a bit posh for us, to be honest. Charlie brought us back to the hotel and helped us to carry all of the presents back to our room. When we were there, I got a text message from Mum and Dad.

They didn't seem as happy as they were when I left. They didn't say anything, but I got the idea that they were probably missing me. And, also, my story was causing a bit of a stir at home. They said that everybody was talking about me. They said that "The Children's Lottery" was the biggest show on the telly, even though the only programmes that had been on so far were the ones telling people what was going to happen. It was really great to receive the message, but I felt so far away. Aunty Ann could see that I had become a bit lonely so she gave me a big hug. Aunty Ann always knows when to give hugs.

----❈ ❈ ❈----

I woke up really early on the day of the first programme. Aunty Ann had jam on toast for her breakfast. She spilt a big blob of jam on her Birmingham City football club shirt. She scooped it off with her finger and offered it to me. I said, "Ugghh! No!", so she just ate it herself. I had ordered some cornflakes, but I was too nervous to eat them.

Charlie came to pick us up in the limousine and took us to the studio. The radio was on in the car and they were talking about the lottery. To be honest, it was getting bigger and bigger all the time. Every time you turned on the TV or radio, it wasn't long before you heard somebody mention the children's lottery.

When we got to the studio, everybody we walked past wanted to shake our hands.

Charlie said goodbye to us. He said that his duties had finished now that the show had started. Aunty Ann was having none of that. She told him that he had to stay. Charlie said that he had to go and drive some other people about town. Aunty went to find Bertie and told him that Charlie had become our good luck charm and that she wanted him to stay.

So, Bertie said that he could stay.

We were taken to a room, called the Green Room. That is the room that you stay in before you are called to go into the studio. There were some nice things to eat laid out on a table, and there was a fridge that had cans of drinks in it that you could just help yourself to. The adults helped themselves to a few little things, but the children didn't.

Chu Li was as quiet and nervous as she was the first time I met her. She had a traditional Chinese dress on that had patterns like flowers, and she had make-up on. She looked a bit funny, to be honest. Aunty Ann told her that she looked really nice. Aunty Ann probably thought that she did. Everybody else was dressed in their best clothes. Aunty Ann was wearing her Birmingham City football club shirt with a stain on the front. I told you that she was a bit different to other adults, didn't I?

We were taken through to the studio and we had to sit behind a table with a microphone on it. Richy was on one side and I was on the other and Chu Li was in the middle. Aunty Ann and Charlie and the other adults sat with the audience.

An announcer came out and said, "Hello," and then he repeated it in lots of different languages. He told us that there were more people tuned into this programme than had ever tuned into any single programme before. He said that there were more people watching us around the world than ever watched man walk on the moon for the first time.

I told you this was getting bigger and bigger, didn't I? They told us that about eighty per cent of the television sets in the world were tuned into this broadcast. Well, I told you that I was a bit nervous before, but now I could feel my tummy rolling around and I could hear myself breathing.

The announcer made a big introduction.

"Ladies and gentlemen, please give a warm welcome to the man behind the Children's Lottery, Lord Stinking Rich Bertie of Stinking Rich Mansion."

Lord Bertie got up and started explaining the show, but I couldn't hear the words he was saying very well. It sounded as though he was shouting down a tunnel. I was so nervous that my knees starting knocking together. This was the first time that I had felt so alone. I wished my Mum and Dad were there, or that Aunty Ann was sitting next to me. I said a "Hail Mary" in my head. That's a prayer that Catholics say a lot. It helped a bit. I felt calmer.

There were going to be three programmes. The first programme was all about getting to know the contestants. During the second programme, one of us would be sent home. And then there was going to be another public vote which decided which one of us would be in the best position to win the jackpot.

Lord Bertie then told us how much the jackpot would be. The news that he gave us made us all gasp. He told us that the winner of the lottery would be given one of his biggest businesses. Then he told us what the cash prize would be. He told us that the winner could win one billion dollars. Yes, one million, million dollars. I imagined my Mum jumping up and down at home, and I could also imagine my Dad trying to keep her calm.

The first round consisted of each of us having one minute to say as many things that we would buy if we had to spend the whole one billion dollars in one day. My mind started whizzing through all of the things I could buy. We each went into a booth and, when the buzzer went, we had a minute to say all of the things that we would buy.

Because Chu Li was so young, they let her Dad help her. So, we all had our minute, and then we came out and they showed the film of what we all said we would buy.

Chu Li's film was shown first. Chu Li and her father were really slow. I felt a bit sorry. They said that they would buy a house and a shop and a farm, but, to be honest, all of the things that they said would not end up being worth half a million, let alone a million millions.

Richy went next and he had a lot more idea of how to spend a lot of money. He said that he would buy himself mansions all over the world. He said he would buy a fleet of sports cars and that he would have swimming pools and stables with his own horses.

Then it was my turn and I crammed as much as I could into my minute. I also said that I would buy big houses and fast cars, but I also said that I would buy aeroplanes and trains, and I said I would buy all of the premiership football clubs and all of the American football clubs. I think my film got the biggest round of applause.

Then Bertie said that there was going to be a phone vote. People from all around the world had to phone a number to say which they thought should go through to the next round.

That was my part over for the day.

I went over to Aunty Ann and Charlie and they thought that I had done enough to stay in. Aunty Ann said that the only thing that stood against me was that I came from a comparatively small country. She said that if people vote for their own country, then it would probably be Richy and Chu Li that would go through because Richy is from America, and they have over a hundred times more people than Britain, and Chu Li is from China, and they have over a million times more people than Britain. All we could do was wait.

Aunty Ann suggested that we have veggie nuggets and chips for dinner. As you can imagine, I thought that would be a very good idea indeed. Did I tell you that I am a vegetarian? Well, I am. I asked Aunty Ann if we were going to have lots of ketchup on it and she said, "of course". Then she gave me one of her special little hugs.

Charlie said that he didn't think that a hotel like this would do veggie nuggets, but he said that there was a diner across the road that he would go to and get them from there. Aunty Ann told Charlie to take me up to our suite. She said that he had done enough work for one day and that he should go and rest while she went to get the chips. Charlie looked confused. It turns out that chips are crisps in America and chips are called fries.

Charlie and I went up to our room and we put on the TV. It seemed like every channel was talking about the Children's Lottery. It seemed that everybody had an opinion as to what we should have spent our billion on. A lot of phone callers thought that the competition was unfair to Chu Li because they thought that she did not understand the idea of the game was that she should say how she would spent the billion in one day if she had to. I looked at Charlie and shrugged my shoulders. He ruffled my hair as he walked past me and he said that Chu Li definitely knew what the rules of the game were because they had the best translators in the world.

Charlie opened up the big glass doors

and walked out onto the balcony, and then he gave out a huge shriek and he said, "oh, no, no, no!" and then he ran back in.

He told me to stay where I was. He told me not to move or go anywhere under any circumstances. He ran out of the suite and went downstairs.

I couldn't stop myself. I ran over to the balcony to see what it was that had upset him so much. I looked down to the streets below and I could see that there had been an accident. I couldn't believe what I was looking at. I could see that someone had been knocked over by a car. I could just make out that it was a woman. There was a man standing over trying to see if she was still alive, and then he moved to one side. I could see that the woman was wearing a Birmingham City football club shirt. I started screaming and crying. I couldn't believe what I was seeing. I had been talking to her only a few minutes earlier. A police car arrived and an ambulance. Their sirens were going off and their lights were flashing. I saw Charlie running across the street, but there were policemen keeping people back. I saw he was trying to let him through, but the more he tried, the more they pushed him back. I fell down on my knees and looked through the bars in the railings on the balcony. I saw them put her onto a stretcher and they lifted her into the back of the ambulance.

As the ambulance sped off down the road, I sat down right where I was and cried and cried. And then Aunty Ann walked in and asked me why I was crying.

"Aunty Ann! Aunty Ann!" I shouted out and ran up to her and threw my arms around her.

"I thought you were dead!" I said, and I hugged her tighter still.

Charlie came running in and he said, "Ann. It's you! You're alive!"

She said, "Well, of course, I'm alive! What's wrong with you?"

Then Charlie explained what had

happened and told her about the woman and the football shirt. Anne was wearing a Cleveland Indians shirt. Charlie asked her how it was that she wasn't wearing her Birmingham City football club shirt that she was wearing when she left. I was too upset to say anything. I just kept hugging Aunty Ann.

What had happened was that when she was leaving the hotel, a woman said that she liked Aunty Ann's shirt, but she had never heard of Birmingham City. Aunty Ann said that she liked the woman's Cleveland Indians shirt and so they swapped there and then in the foyer. I told you she was a bit mad, didn't I?

Charlie gave Aunty Ann a big hug as well. He told her that he was worried out of his skin when he thought that it was her that had been hit.

None of us felt like eating the chips. We just sat around being quiet. We had the telly on, but I don't think any of us were really watching it. I just kept on thinking of how a life could be over in no time at all. I kept thinking of how lucky we were and I kept thinking of how unlucky the poor woman was that had been run over. It was obvious that we were all worrying about the woman so much that we couldn't rest. So Charlie took us down to the hospital to find out how she was.

We had to wait for a long time and it was a bit frightening because there were quite a few angry people there. You could tell that some were drunk and some were down on their luck. When the doctors did come out, they had some good news for us. There was no permanent damage. She had hurt her shoulder quite badly and she had broken her leg as well. So she really was quite lucky. I know that sounds silly because she was hurt so badly, but really, she was lucky because it could easily have been so much worse.

We felt a bit better on the way home. In fact, we felt so much better that we stopped at a diner and had veggie nuggets and chips with lots of tomato ketchup.

You will never guess what happened then. I told you that the Children's Lottery had become really big. It was in all of the newspapers, it seemed as though it was on every radio station, and it was certainly on just about every TV channel in America. Well, as I was dipping my nuggets in my ketchup, a woman and her daughter came up to me and asked me if I would give them my autograph! Can you believe that? Until a couple of weeks ago, I was the quiet kid walking around the playground by myself, and now I had people coming up to me asking me for my autograph - in America!

Soon, other people started coming up to me and they asked me for my autograph as well. Before we knew it, things were getting out of hand and people were getting quite agitated.

Charlie decided that we should leave, and he guided us out of the back door and drove us back to the hotel.

America is a great place at night. There

are lots of different coloured lights, and the people are always busy, and there are loads of cars beeping their horns.

When we got back to the hotel, I could see that everybody was looking at me. Some people were staring at me and some were just sneaking glances over their shoulders. But everybody went quiet as I walked past. Everything had changed. I was public property. And I liked it. In fact, I loved it. I wanted to take a bow, but something stopped me.

Aunty Ann tucked me up in bed and we said our prayers together. We said an "Our Father" and three "Hail Marys". They're prayers that Catholics say. Then we said "God bless Mum and Dad and all of the family". Then we said "God bless all of our friends and everyone that we know". Then we said a special prayer for the woman who got knocked down in the car accident. Aunty Ann told me to get a good night's sleep because tomorrow I would find out if I was going home with a million dollars or whether I was still in the Children's Lottery and I had a chance of winning one of the biggest businesses in the world, plus one billion dollars.

I kept thinking about how much money a billion dollars really is. Once I had spent one million dollars, I would still have nine hundred and ninety nine thousand, nine hundred and ninety nine million dollars left. That's because in America a billion is a million millions. In Britain, a billion is a thousand millions.

"Oh, I don't know," I thought to myself. Maybe I had got that wrong. Anyway, I had spent so much time working it out that I became really tired and I drifted off to sleep.

---- ❋ ❋ ❋ ----

We had an early call to go back into the studio first thing in the morning. Charlie called to collect us and Aunty Ann gave him a kiss on his cheek. He took us down some back stairs that only a few people knew about. The Children's Lottery frenzy had just grown and grown. Charlie said that it would take us hours to get past the crowds in the front of the hotel.

The three contestants had to sit up on the pedestal places again. Chu Li seemed tired of all the attention, but Richy loved it. I couldn't say much about that because I was enjoying it as well. But I liked Richy less every time I saw him. He strutted about the place as though he was the King of all that he saw. He was bad enough when I first met him, but now that people were clamouring to ask him for his autograph, he was unbearable.

He was wearing a suit that had sequins on it! I mean, I ask you! What kind of lad wears a suit with sequins on it? And when he walked onto the set, he brought his dog with him. It was a little toy poodle that had been dyed pink and he had a collar that was covered in diamonds. Richy sat his dog on a little velvet cushion and the audience started to scream and shout. It made me want to be sick. It's a shame I didn't feel sick. If I had felt sick, I would have walked over to him, put my fingers down my throat and been sick all over him. Forget I said that. It wasn't even a very nice thing to think, let alone add into my story.

Bertie was introduced and he read out some messages from around the world. It seemed that people from every continent had sent messages for us.

The Prime Minister of Britain sent a message saying he thought the programme was the best programme ever and he hoped that we were all having a good time.

The President of the United States of America said that the programme made him proud to be American.

There were other world leaders who sent messages and also religious leaders sent some. They wanted us to use our money wisely.

All day long there were people phoning

up the television station saying that it was wrong that children should be given so much money. It seemed that the whole world was divided into two by the Children's Lottery. Half the world thought it was the most exciting thing that they had ever seen, and the other half thought that it was dreadful. The half that thought that it was dreadful got really angry and they made all kinds of threats. Some of the threats were so bad that Bertie said he was going to make sure that a bodyguard would go everywhere with us until the final show was over.

Then came a message that each of us really loved. It was the best part of the whole experience so far. There was a message on the screen from our homes.

Chu Li went first. Her grandmother came on the screen and spoke to her in Chinese, and you could tell that Chu Li was really pleased to hear from her because she started crying. Some other people from her village came on to wish her well. The audience applauded. I think they were pleased to see Chu Li looking so happy.

Then, my parents came on. I know just how Chu Li felt because I really wanted to cry. There's nothing like seeing a film of somebody to make you realise just how far away you are from them. Dad said that nobody in his charity wanted to talk about themselves or their problems. All they wanted to talk about was the Children's Lottery. My Mum told me that she had been so nervous that she just kept knitting all of the time. She told me she had a new jumper waiting for me. Everybody in the audience laughed. I think that maybe "jumper" means something else in America. Then I had another surprise. My Head Teacher came on and told me that everybody was thinking of me and wished me well. Then my Teacher came on and she was really nice. She said that she had saved all of my homework for me so that I had lots of work to come back to. Then my last brilliant surprise was my whole class shouting, "Hip,

hip, hooray!" three times for me.

In no time at all, I had gone from being the boy that nobody would choose as their partner in PE to being one of the most popular people in the world. It was as though I had become a pop star or a football player.

Then Richy's family came on. His gran had written a poem for him. It went like this.

"My heart strains when I am away from you.

My hands feel sore when they cannot reach out and touch you.

My power withers a little every hour that we are apart.

You are my air.

You are my water.

You are my food.

I feel that I cannot live a moment longer without you, my darling grandson.

I love you."

Well, the American audience absolutely loved that! They cheered and shouted and some of them got handkerchieves out of their pockets to wipe tears from their eyes. I had never seen anything like it. I thought it was a bit sickly sweet, to be honest.

Aunty Ann and Charlie had taken their handkerchieves out and were pretending to cry, and they were leaning on each other's shoulders and pretending that they were crying their eyes out. They obviously thought it was a bit false as well.

Charlie and Aunty Ann were really hitting it off and Aunty Ann wasn't one to let the grass grow under her feet, so she asked Charlie if he would like to be her boyfriend. Charlie said that he would like that more than anything else in the world. So they became all lovey dovey. I was absolutely delighted for Aunty Ann. She was probably the happiest person I knew, but I'd never seen her as happy as this. It was really nice to see the two of them all loved up. You'd think that they had won the lottery! Well, I suppose they had, in a way.

The next thing that Bertie said was that he was going to ask each of us if we wanted to go on with the Children's Lottery, or if we wanted to go home with one million dollars. Now, you wouldn't think that anyone would give up on the chance of being a billionnaire. But Chu Li and her parents actually said that they had had enough. It seems that all of the attention was too much for her. She didn't like the bright lights or the big city. All they wanted to do was get back to their little village. Chu Li's father thanked Bertie and the Children's Lottery, but he said that they were simple people and they wanted to get back to their home. I just couldn't believe it. I couldn't think of turning my back on a billion dollars. I couldn't imagine anybody I knew turning their back on a billion dollars. And just because they were homesick! It seems that Chu Li's parents thought that a billion dollars was too much for them to cope with. I couldn't understand it myself. Could you turn your back on the chance of a billion dollars?

Could you think of anybody you knew turning their back on the chance of a billion dollars?

They lifted Chu Li onto a big chair and four huge men lifted her up and carried her away. Thousands of small pieces of silver paper were dropped from the ceiling and indoor fireworks were let off all over the studio. Chu Li was given a cheque for a million dollars.

And then there were two. The Children's Lottery winner was going to be me or Richy. As Chu Li was taken from the studio and the sounds subsided, a calm fell over the whole studio and the lights dimmed. Bertie stepped up to the microphone and then he gave us our next task.

On the third and final programme, we were told, we had to tell everybody about ourselves and our lives and what we thought our lives would be like if we won the Children's Lottery. I spent a restless night in my hotel, and I'm sure Richy did too.

On programme three, Richy went first.

He told everybody about how fabulous he was. He told them about all of the horse riding medals that he had won. He told them about the awards that he had won at school and he told them that he had a house with a swimming pool and servants. Then he said that, if he was a billionnaire, he would have his own personal chef and he would be chauffeur driven everywhere and that he would have his own personal McDonalds that nobody else would be able to eat in.... except his dog. He said that he would have his own bowling alley and that he would retire from work before he even started. All of the audience cheered and shouted and they started chanting, "Richy! Richy! Richy! Richy!"

And then it was my turn. I didn't know what to say, to be honest. I looked over to Aunty Ann and Charlie and they put their thumbs up and encouraged me. I said a little prayer and asked God to help me do the right thing.

So then I just stood up and told them all

about my life. I told them that I love books and that my Mum sometimes brings me a whole bagful at one go. I told them about my favourites. I told them how much I like the Vlad the Drac books. I told them how much I like Jacqueline Wilson and JK Rowling. I love Philip Putnam. I told them that my best Harry Potter book was The Chamber of Secrets. I told them about my class and my teacher. I told them that being here was the best thing that had ever happened to my family. I told them about my Mum tucking her dress into her knickers. I said that a billion was really too big for me to understand. I told them that if I started counting now, I would probably be a very old man before I reached a billion. I told them that I was more concerned about having to look after Lord Bertie's business. I told them that I would most like to be happy and to make my family proud of me. I said that I would pay for somebody to do my parents' work so that they could retire. And then I sat down. There was just a bit of ordinary applause. But there was no shouting out or cheering like there was for Richy.

Then Lord Bertie dropped something of a bombshell. He reminded us that, at the beginning, he had told us that nothing was as it seems. Lord Bertie said that the votes from around the world would account for thirty three percent of the overall decision as to who won the billion dollars and the company. He told us that thirty three percent of the vote would go to each of his brothers, whom he had learned to trust implicitly. And if there was a tie at the end of that, then he would have the casting vote.

Lord Bertie called for his two brothers to come on to the stage. Charlie squeezed my hand, and Aunty Ann's.

"Excuse me for a few moments," he said. "I have a job to do."

And with that, he stood up and walked on to the stage. Aunty Ann and I looked at the stage and then at each other, and then we looked around us and then back to the stage. It turned out that Charlie was not a chauffeur after all. He was Lord Bertie's brother!

Lord Bertie said that he had arranged for his brothers to pose as chauffeurs so that they could get to find out what we were really like before casting their vote. Charlie and George, his other brother, stood on the stage by Lord Bertie. Aunty Ann never said a word (that's a first!). She just sat and stared at Charlie. I couldnt' believe it. I would never have guessed in a million years. Charlie stood there looking all smug. He looked all around him whilst Lord Bertie was talking and he threw a big smile in our direction from time to time.

First of all, Lord Bertie said that he was going to reveal the results of the phone vote. It was a nerve wracking time because my whole future depended upon the outcome of the next few minutes.

It seemed that more people on the planet had voted on this programme than had voted for anything else in the world. It took ages for them to reveal all of the votes. It was a bit like the Eurovision Song Contest except this wasn't just in Europe, it was from all over the world.

As the votes were revealed, sometimes Richy would go in front and then sometimes I would overtake. Richy was just in front of me when it came down to the final vote. And that was from America. I said that he was bound to win it, but Aunty Ann said, "You never know."

When they revealed the American vote, Richy had a lot more than me. He jumped up and punched the air.

He shouted, "Yes! Yes!" and pranced about the stage like a bullfighter.

He stood with both hands in the air whilst the crowd cheered and clapped. I felt really sad. I felt as though I had let everyone down. Aunty Ann put her arm around me and told me to keep my chin up because it wasn't all over yet.

They turned the votes into percentages and it turned out that Richy was eight percent ahead.

I had done more arithmetic in the last few days than I had ever done in my life. I wasn't at all sure what that vote meant. I looked at Aunty Ann, but I don't think she was too sure either. But she told me I was still in with a chance. A picture came into my mind of me walking up to my Mum, if I missed out on a billion dollars, and telling her how sorry I was.

Lord Bertie called upon Charlie to cast his vote. Charlie walked up to the podium and told the world what he thought about me. To be honest, I think he spoke more about Aunty Ann than he did about me. He told the world that the last few days had led him to look upon us as two of the nicest people he had met in his entire life. He told the world about Aunty Ann giving bacon and sausage to strangers. He told them about how his heart sank when he thought that Aunty Ann had been run over. He told them that eating French fries and chatting with the two of us was more enjoyable than eating the finest food in the best restaurants with anybody else. Then he told his brother and the world that he was giving every single vote that he had to me, and that, if he had any more to give, then he would gladly give them as well.

The audience applauded with a fair amount of enthusiasm. I think that if there is one thing that Americans like more than someone who is American, then it is someone who is winning!

Charlie went back and stood by Lord Bertie and George went to the podium. Lord Bertie said that the production team had done the maths. He told us that if George awarded twenty five or more of his votes to Richy then he would be the winner. If George awarded twenty four or fewer of his votes to Richy then I would be the winner.

The lights in the studio went down and the background music faded. The spotlight shone upon George, and it was time at last to find out who would become the richest boy on earth. George waited for a moment without speaking and the world waited with him. And then he spoke.

"Like my brother, Charlie, I have spent the last few days undercover. I have been trying to find out what kind of a person Richy is. I have been trying to think what kind of a job he would make of being in charge of one of the biggest companies in the world. And I have got to tell my fellow Americans and citizens of the world that I cannot think of one single human being that I would less like to see inherit my brother's wealth. That young man. And his family! They are the most arrogant people I have ever met in my life! Why, they treated me worse than they treated their dog. And even the dog is the most vile animal I have ever met in my life!"

The dog ran up to him and started biting his leg. The audience gave a gasp. George swung his leg round and the little pink poodle went flying into the air. The crowd laughed and cheered as the dog scampered back to his owners.

George said, "Why, I wouldn't give one single vote to that family if they were the last family on earth!"

The crowd applauded George, and Richy and his mother started hurling abuse at the stage. The audience seemed very shocked indeed. When Security came to carry them away, the crowd started cheering.

Lord Bertie shouted out my name and declared me the winner. Aunty Ann and I hugged each other as though our lives depended on it. Everybody in the audience wanted to shake my hand or pat me on the back. It took me about five minutes to make my way to the stage.

When I finally got there, I was brought over to a chair by Lord Bertie. He asked me how I felt. I just shook my head. I couldn't think of a single thing to say. I had a huge smile on my face. I couldn't stop smiling.

Lord Bertie told me that I was the richest boy in the world and he asked me what I was going to do with all the money. I told him that I wanted to make my family happy and to make them proud of me. I waved my hands in the air like a mad thing and everybody laughed. Bertie explained that the company I had inherited would be looked after by trustees until I was twenty five. He said that that meant that I would get all of the money from it but that I wouldn't have to do any of the work.

I said, "Oh. That sounds good." And everybody laughed again.

He asked me what the very first thing was that I was going to do. I told him that I was going to go to the toilet. And then everybody laughed again!

Charlie walked onto the stage with a giant cheque for ONE BILLION dollars and presented it to me. Loads of photographers came in and knelt down by the foot of the stage and a blanket of flash bulbs filled

84

the room. Thousands of tiny pieces of gold paper fell from the roof. A fanfare struck up and my world was changed forever. With the interest from the bank, I was a hundred pounds richer every time I blinked my eyes.

It seemed like a very long time indeed until Aunty Ann and I were finally alone back in our room. The first thing we did was phone home and really just listened to Mum screaming on the other end. After a while, Charlie came to visit us. Gone was his chauffeur's uniform, and in its place was an immaculate dark Armani suit.

Aunty Ann said, "Don't you deceive me like that again. Do you understand? I never want to hear of you trying to pull the wool over my eyes again."

She took him by the hand and led him into the room.

"And I certainly won't stand for that kind of behaviour after we are married," she said.

"I didn't know we were getting married,"

Charlie said.

"Oh, yes, you did," said Aunty Ann.

"I guess I did," said Charlie, "but I was just waiting for you to tell me."

They smiled at each other and started kissing.

"Uggghhh!!! Excuse me!" I said. "It's time for me to go and watch telly in my room."

I went and turned the telly on, but, to be honest, not much of it registered. My head was just buzzing with ideas.

----❄ ❄ ❄----

Part of the deal was that I had to do a few things as the winner. I had to have my photograph taken quite a lot and meet a few people. I had to meet the trustees of the company. I had to meet with financial advisors. Oh, and they told me that I had to go and have dinner with the President. I thought that they meant the President of the company, but they actually meant the

86

President of the United States of America.

The next few days, well weeks or months, really, were something of a blur. They brought me newspapers from virtually every country in the world and my picture was on the front page of every single one. I was probably the most famous boy on the planet. One thing that I wasn't ready for was gifts. It seemed that everybody wanted to give me gifts. I got loads and loads and loads of chocolate. Honestly, there was more than you could eat in an entire lifetime. And people sent so many sweets. It seemed as though every sweet shop in the world wanted me to have their sweets. I probably had enough sweets to fill an entire sweet shop myself. People sent me pens, mirrors, ornaments, clothes. One company sent me a box of cigars. I have no idea what they were thinking of! People sent me so many different things, it would take me forever to list them all. One company sent me ointment, for heaven's sake! Why, on earth, would a company want to

send it to a boy? Perhaps the most amazing thing that I was sent was a sports car. I just couldn't understand why so many people felt the need to send me free gifts. After all, I was now the richest boy in the whole wide world. I suppose there are just some things that I will never make sense of.

Dinner with the President was fun. We had a police escort. There was just me, Aunty Ann and Charlie, the President, the President's wife and their daughter. It turned out that they had watched all three of the programmes on the telly. They had felt sorry for Chu Li. I told them I thought that she would be better off without all of the attention that I'd been getting. The President told me that he was a betting man. He said that he only liked to bet when he thought that he was on to a winner, and he said that he would bet that I would do well with my new life.

I had to do some interviews for television and then I had to do some photo shoots for magazines. I fell into my new life like falling off a log. It was a piece of cake. I had never really liked to be the centre of attention but I somehow seemed to relish it now. Wherever I was, if there was another human being present, then they wanted to stare at me. It might sound awful, but I quite liked it. I used to love dressing up in the clothes that my mum bought for me from Oxfam, but, to be honest, I liked dressing up in designer gear just as much. It's just the same, really. It's just a few thousand dollars more expensive.

Anyway, that was America. Then it was time to go home. Aunty Ann had met the man of her dreams and she was happier now than she had ever been in her life. I couldn't have been more happy for her. But now I was ready to go home. This had all been a wonderful adventure. I had grown to really quite enjoy posh hotels and room service. But I really was ready for home. I was really looking forward to being at home with Mum and Dad and being back in my own bed! Charlie wasn't able to come with us because he had work to do. He was only going to be a few weeks behind us, though.

We went to the airport in an old truck that was driven by Lord Bertie. He shouted at virtually every motorist that we passed. Aunty Ann and I were laughing out loud as he threw us from side to side. He was using so many swear words that Aunty Ann put her hands over my ears. Lord Bertie apologised and then he started again! Aunty Ann asked him why he hadn't got a chauffeur and he said that wouldn't be nearly as much fun. I asked him why it made him so angry if it was such fun.

"I'm not angry," he said. "I'm just enjoying myself."

The flight home was as you might imagine - first class! Aunty Ann didn't bother with the champagne this time. She just had a snooze instead. I sat awake, looking forward to running up to my Mum and throwing my arms around her. And I was looking forward to dumping my bags down and jumping onto my bed. I couldn't wait to get back to school. I couldn't wait to see all of my friends and my teachers.

It's great arriving first class at an airport. They go and get your luggage for you and you don't have to wait ages at the carousel. The first thing we did when we got back was to phone Mum, of course. But she told us that we couldn't go home. I couldn't understand why , at first, but it turned out that there were so many reporters in our street that the police had been called. There were hundreds and hundreds of people that had travelled from all over the country who just wanted to see me. Blimey! I wasn't quite ready for that. I thought it was just in America that people would be like that. Mum said that they had booked into a secret hotel. So Aunty Ann and I arranged to go and join them.

It wasn't the homecoming that I had looked forward to. I'd had enough of hotels, to be honest. As we walked past a TV set in the airport, I saw myself on the telly. It was one of the interviews that I had given in America. My picture was on the cover of almost every magazine on every shelf. When someone spotted who I was, they shouted out, and, within seconds, I was being mobbed by everybody in the entire airport.

Aunty Ann somehow got me into a taxi, and we made our way off to the hotel. It seemed as though I wasn't leaving the madness behind, but that it was coming with me.

It was great to see Mum and Dad again. The hotel was brilliant because it was like having your own little house inside the hotel. There were four bedrooms and a living room and a games room. That night, I lay down on the settee next to my Mum and watched telly. It wasn't home, but it was the next best thing.

I couldn't go back to school on the next day because I had to meet with my new financial advisor that Lord Bertie had arranged. But, as it turns out, I couldn't have gone back to school anyway, because there were thousands of reporters there. It was a shame, really. I would have loved to have gone back to school. It seemed like a lifetime ago when I would have loved to have a day off!

When the financial advisor came to see us, he was really nice. I wasn't quite ready for everybody else, though. There was a head of Security (and his team). There was head of Public Relations (and her team). And there was head of Business Affairs (and, yes, you've guessed it, his team). Dad made them wait outside. He said that we would see them one at a time. My first appointment was with my financial advisor. My Mum asked him if we could afford to stay in the hotel, and he told her that we could afford to buy it. And ten thousand like it! We were beginning to realise just how rich we really were.

I told him that I didn't really want all of the other people, but he explained how necessary they all were. He said that security was really important because there were people who would want to hurt me now, just because I was who I was. One of the biggest bombshells was that he said I would have to buy a new house. I couldn't believe it. I said that there was no way that I was moving, but he explained that I would need a house with much more security. He said that I would need electronic gates and cameras and electric fences. He said that I would need an estate with accommodation for all of the staff and room for a business centre.

I told him that I just wanted to go home to my own house, with my own bed and be with my own family. Dad said that I should have thought of that when I bought the lottery ticket. He could see that he had really upset me and he apologised straight away.

He said, "Look, it doesn't matter where we live. We will all be together and wherever we are, it will soon become home."

I think that our financial advisor thought

that we were a bit odd. I suppose he thought that everybody wanted to live in a big mansion with swimming pools and lakes and stables for the horses. I suppose that I would get used to it in time. I just wasn't ready for it, that's all. I was told that I wouldn't be able to go back to school for a few weeks.

We signed control of the business over to the trustees so there was nothing else for it. It was time to start spending.

I arranged for lots of sweets to be sent to every child in school and Dad phoned the Head Teacher and asked him to make a list of everything that he wanted for the school. He said that they could do with a new computer, and we told him that he could have a new computer for every child in the school, if he wanted one. Dad said that he just went quiet on the other end of the phone.

We are a small family, but we did have some distant relatives and we weren't part of a large social circle. So what we decided to do was to make a list of all our relatives, no matter how distant. Then we made a list of all our nice neighbours and friends. Then Mum and Dad added the names of people that they liked from their work. They also made a list of all of the poor people that Dad helped with his charity. So, really, we went and collected everybody in the world that we liked. We drove them around in a limousine. We were house hunting. I wanted to buy every single one of them the house of their dreams.

We went on just about the most amazing spending spree that Britain had ever seen. We drove down people's streets. Then they came running out and screaming and shouting and jumping up and down and they piled into the rows and rows of stretched limousines. Then we drove around looking at houses that were for sale. We would pull up outside and shout, "Who fancies this house?" And when somebody said they did, we would say, "It's yours!" We bought houses the way children buy sweets.

We went round to loads of different

shops, and, to begin with, we picked things up to see if we wanted them, but, after a while, we just started picking anything up and saying, "We'll have that! We'll have that! We'll have that!" And before long, we didn't even bother picking things up. We just pointed to them and shopkeepers ran around picking them up for us.

We spent a few weeks looking at different mansions. We wanted to buy the first one we looked at, but Mr Burns (did I tell you that's what our financial advisor was called? Anyway, that's his name, and he's really nice.) made us look at a few before we decided. I'm glad he did, because we kept on seeing ones that we liked even better.

I told Mr Burns that I was worried about our new home being too far away from school. He said that I could always get a helicopter to school. I asked him where it would land, but it turned out he was only joking anyway. I asked him if I could have a helicopter if I wanted one, and he said I could have a thousand if I wanted. He told me that I was about fifty thousand pounds richer when I went to bed at night than I was when I got up in the morning. And then he said I was about fifty thousand pounds richer when I got up in the morning than I was when I went to bed. I was only just beginning to realise (again) how rich I was.

I wasn't able to go back to school just yet because of all the press. But, what we decided to do instead was to have a day out for the whole school. Mr Burns arranged for Alton Towers to be closed for a day just so that all the children in my school could meet me there for a fun day out. It was brilliant! You've never seen so many happy children in your life. We went from ride to ride and just jumped on without having to queue up. It was brilliant! Brilliant! Brilliant! Brilliant! Everybody wanted to be my friend. I was on top of the world. All of the stalls and restaurants were open and everybody could go up to them and have anything that they wanted. They could have candy floss or burgers or coke or anything and they could have anything, absolutely anything, that they wanted from the souvenir stands. It was the most fabulous, fabulous time. People couldn't run from one ride to another fast enough, and the teachers and parents enjoyed it as much as the children. Even my Dad was going on rides. Mum didn't, but she had a good excuse. She had a baby in her tummy. That little baby didn't know it yet, but he or she was going to be born into one of the richest families in the world.

I kept on patting Mum's tummy and saying, "You don't know how lucky you are, do you?" And then I would give her little bump a kiss.

That day was probably the best day of my life. I came up with another great idea as well. I decided to buy all of the teachers in our school a brand new sports car each. I ordered them all to be delivered first thing in the morning so that, when the teachers

arrived at school, they wouldn't be able to get into the car park because all the new cars were there. Ha ha! I would have given anything to have been able to be there to see their faces when they realised that the sports cars were for them!

My publicity people kept the press away from me most of the time. After several weeks had passed, I arranged to do one major television interview, though. It was the biggest talk show on the telly. Robbie Williams was on the show. That was Mum's favourite singer. She came with me so that she could meet him. He was really nice to her. He kissed her and picked her up and showed her his tattoos. When he found out that she was having a baby, he even gave the little bump a kiss as well.

The interview was brilliant. I used to be quite shy, but I had become the exact opposite. I really enjoyed the limelight. I found that I could make people laugh. The interviewer asked me what the best thing

103

was about being rich. And I said that my Mum got to be kissed by Robbie Williams. The audience all laughed. He asked me what the best thing was that I had bought since I had all the money.

I said, "Oooh, that's hard. It might be the houses or it might be the cars. It might be every X-Box game in the world. But," I said, "actually, it's probably the sweets and the chocolate."

The audience laughed again, and I loved the whole experience.

I was on cloud nine. Today had probably been the best day I had had since the day out at Alton Towers. On the way back to the hotel, I asked the driver to stop off at McDonalds for tea. I just had a yearning for a veggie burger and Mum agreed. We pulled up outside McDonalds and I had a big surprise. I saw one of the boys from my class sitting in the chair by the window so I went in to say hello to him. When I got in there, I had an even bigger surprise. There were other children from my class in there. In fact, when I looked round, I realised that the whole class was in there. I couldn't believe it. One of the boys was having his birthday party in there and he hadn't invited me. He looked really embarrassed when he saw me standing there. In fact, they all did. I ran back to the car, crying. I just couldn't believe that they would have a party without inviting me. Especially when you think of everything I had done for them! The boy came out and said that he didn't think I would be interested in McDonalds. But I just told the driver to drive us home. But, even then, I said "back to the hotel" because it wasn't really home, was it?

My Mum and Dad tried to comfort me, but I had never felt more sad or more lonely in my life. All I could see was my whole class enjoying themselves at a party and me not being invited! I closed my eyes, but I could still see them all.

----❋❋❋----

Mr Burns quickly grew to be someone that we all came to rely upon. He asked us to have an important meeting and he had prepared some things for us to talk about. He had found an ideal mansion for us and showed us what it looked like on the computer. It was fabulous. It had a lake that was big enough for water sports, like jet ski-ing, and it had a place for quad bikes and scrambling. The indoor swimming pool had slides and the outside pool was heated. It was still in Britain (I can't tell you where exactly - for security reasons), but it was a long way from where we lived. It meant that we would have to leave our family and friends. It meant that Mum and Dad would have to leave their work, and it would mean that I would have to start a new school.

None of us really wanted to change. The new house was amazing. It had its own cinema and stables. It was a big decision. The way I felt about the children in my class made me feel as though I didn't care if I never saw any of them ever again, but the thought of never seeing any of them again made me really sad. I think Mr Burns knew what I was going through. He said that if I did make friends with the children in my class then this mansion would be a great place for them to visit or even stay for a holiday. I must admit that did sound like fun.

I asked him what school I would go to and he said that he had been thinking about that as well. He said that I could arrange for tutors to come to me, but that seemed a bit like hard work. And it seemed a bit lonely. Then he told us about Angus Down. It was a public school. It was one of the most expensive public schools in the world. All of the children there were rich, so I wouldn't be the odd one out. Their parents were film stars, pop stars, politicians, footballers and even royalty. He said that I could choose whether to be a day boy or a boarder. He said that it would be close enough to travel to, but that if I wanted to I could go by helicopter because there was a place for it to land.

Life was full of decisions now. We spent a day looking at the new mansion and we spent a day looking at Angus Down. I found out something interesting. Do you know why they call "public school" "public school" and not "private school"? It's because, before schools were invented, teachers used to go to your home to teach you. A few people who weren't quite rich enough to pay for a teacher just for their children decided to get together and start a school. This meant that members of the public could send their children to school, but, if you wanted a private education, your children stayed at home.

Angus Down was the most fantastic place in the world. All of the lessons I saw looked like fun. The science lab was amazing. I saw some boys playing rugby and I thought I might give that a go. They even had a boxing club. I don't mind a fight. Did I tell you that? I know you shouldn't, but, if you're in a boxing ring with gloves and a head guard and a referee, it would be all right. They even had a rock climbing wall. And they go off on camps and they do real rock climbing and they go canoeing. This was the easiest decision that I would ever make in my life.

Our new house soon became a home, just like Dad said it would. Aunty Ann came to stay with us. The plan was that she would come and live with us (well, we had enough room) until after the baby was born. And then she would stay for a while to help Mum with the baby. Charlie came to stay as well. They had plans to get married in the summer. The wedding was the only thing that Aunty Ann ever talked about. It was quite funny really, because every time she spoke about the wedding, I could see Mum and Dad look at each other and smile. Aunty Ann said that she wanted me to be a page boy. She told me that I would have to wear a kilt. I told her that I would love to.

She said, "You don't really have to. I was

only joking."

I had changed. I liked the new me. I was the same, really, only more confident.

I started off as a day boy at Angus Down, but, after a week, I asked Mum and Dad if I could board. They were cool about it.

Angus Down was great. I could really be me there. I became much more sporty. We have houses, and I'm in Churchill. But there are also Montgomery, Henry V and Prince Albert. We call Montgomery boys "Monties", Henry V boys, "Hals" and Prince Albert's are called "Berties". We're called "Winnies". I don't know why. I suppose I should ask somebody really.

I've started playing the guitar. We've got a really whizzo guitar master and my new best friend is called Concordo. Everybody calls him Connie and his Dad is one of the best rock guitarists in the world and he has come in and given us lessons as well. They've got a villa in Tuscany and I might go there in

the hols. Connie is great. We do everything together. We've even started writing songs together. Connie is the youngest boy ever to be a Maddie. To be a Maddie, you have to climb out of your dorm window. You have to climb from balcony to balcony around the quad. Then you have to climb onto Madeleine Bridge and jump into "old Moses". That's the river. It's really dangerous. You've got to be really brave to do it. It has only ever been done by Heffers or Seniors before. The masters would have a screaming fit if they found out.

I've started running as well. I came first in the Lord Coe Cup. I love running. I could run all day and still want to run some more. Connie and I often run together after evensong. We could keep running until ten o'clock at night, but the hot water goes off at nine thirty. So, as we have yet to disregard all concern for personal welfare, we tend to be back by nine thirty! We can have a shower every evening, but Churchill's bath times are Wednesday and

Outstanding Achie

WINNER
1st
Lord Coe Cup

Lord Coe Cup

113

Sunday. Both Connie and I are bath people. We tend to use heaps of bubble bath and we lather it up a treat and have a good old splash around. Connie's parents are away a lot of the time, so we tend to spend a lot of time at my house on ref breaks.

That first semester at Angus was absolutely top. Connie and I started playing cricket and the most fabulous thing happened at the Fathers versus Boys annual challenge. I bowled out the Prime Minister! It was on the same day that Mum was due to have the baby. She got so excited, I thought she was going to give birth right outside the Pavilion. When I went to field at long stop, Mum made everybody laugh by coming over to give me a big hug. She had bare feet and a huge belly and she was holding her hat down so that it didn't blow away. Everybody likes my Mum. She brought my pastoral master a pot of home-made jam. I think that made them friends for life. All of my pals like my Mum. She's the best.

----❋❋❋----

That all happened during the wonderful summer of my first term at Angus. And then Issy was born. Isabelle is my baby sister. When Issy was born, it was like winning the lottery all over again. Everything changed. Issy is a Down's baby. If you don't know what that means, don't worry. I didn't either. But, I'm something of an expert now, so I'll tell you all about Issy and all about Down's. Don't worry if you are having a Down's brother or sister. It's not the end of the world, but be prepared. Everything does change. I suppose everything changes every time a new baby is born. You're never the same family any more, are you? I wasn't the same. I wasn't an only child any more. I have Issy now. I'm a big brother, all of a sudden.

Issy was so tiny and beautiful when she was born. We loved her the moment we saw her. You don't stop loving a child when

you find out they have Down's. You probably love them more. When we found out, we were shocked, but it didn't stop us being really happy. But, we did have concerns about the future. At first, you think that you've been really unlucky and that she has been really unlucky. But there is so much love that it blows all of these feelings away.

The night that Issy was born was like a dream. Mum had been in hospital for quite a while, so we knew when she was going to be born. Aunty Ann and Uncle Charlie were there. At least Issy's birth stopped Aunty Ann from talking about the wedding. Aunty Ann was brilliant (she always is!). She sang songs to Issy from the moment she was born. She kept singing a song about a "brand new combine harvester". It was really silly and, the more people laughed, the more she sang. I took a photograph of Aunty Ann singing to Issy and the whole family is laughing. That was the happiest moment of my life. And that photograph is my favourite photograph in the whole world.

We had more questions than answers, so Mr Burns arranged for us to go and meet some people with Down's to find out what they were like. He was just the right person to have around (he always is!).

Issy was just a few months old when we went to the Acton Down's Group. We met people there of all ages and we spoke to them and members of their families. It was a really uplifting day. It made us all feel so positive. Aunty Ann and Uncle Charlie came with us. Lord Bertie came as well because he was over from America for Aunty Ann's wedding.

Sarah and Mike were the first people we met. Their baby, Ben, was there. They told us that he had only just learnt to walk and so he was making up for lost time. He had just thrown his Dad's mobile phone down the toilet. Ben thought that was very funny and we did too! Sarah said that it was no use trying to tell him off because you could never stay angry at him for long. He knows that if he makes you laugh, you can't stay mad at him for long. Lord Bertie was sitting on a big comfy chair in the corner of the room and Ben went over to him and kissed him. We all laughed. Lord Bertie didn't know quite what to make of it. Mike explained to us that Ben didn't understand the rules. Ben might just decide to go up to a stranger on the bus and give him a kiss. He said that most people were like Lord Bertie and didn't know what to make of it, but, he said that usually people smiled. He told us that Ben was such a lovely little boy, he wouldn't swap him for all the tea in China.

We met Emma, who was six. She shook hands with us and said, "I'm very pleased to meet you." Then she stepped back behind her Mum. Her Mum laughed.

She said, "That's not the real Emma at all."

She told us that Emma was a real whirlwind, who was first up every morning. She was at a mainstream school and was eager

121

to get involved in everything. She took all of the same classes as all of the other children. Emma's Mum said that all of the other children knew that she was different, but that they had no problems. They all seemed to play nicely with her. She said that Emma was a regular child who got herself drinks and played on the computer. She could brush her teeth and get herself ready for bed. Emma's Mum said that she was a little bit worried about the future because she didn't know what the future would hold. But I told her that none of us knew that, and everyone was quick to agree.

Rebecca was fourteen. Her Mum said that she was aware that she had Down's Syndrome. She said that Rebecca went through a phase a few years ago when she tried to use it to her advantage. If her Mum asked her to go and get her coat, Rebecca would say, "I can't. I've got Down's Syndrome." That made us all laugh, and Rebecca laughed along with us.

Rebecca's Mum said, "That's all stopped now. She's a pretty good teenager. She has the occasional tantrum, but then, she wouldn't be a teenager without that, would she?"

You could tell that Rebecca liked to see us all laughing. Aunty Ann asked Rebecca if she liked school. She said she loved it. Her Mum said that school was one big party for her. Well, she said everything was, really. Rebecca was in a mainstream school and she had a full time Special Needs Assistant who helped her with everything. She wasn't particularly friendly with one person in school, but she was generally very popular. For her fifteenth birthday she was planning a birthday party in her room with disco lights and a Karaoke machine. Rebecca regularly announced that she had a new boyfriend. Sometimes, she would tell the boy. Other times, she wouldn't.

Melanie seemed to me to be a quiet, thoughtful person. She was twenty seven years old and she had Down's Syndrome. She told us that she loved to sing and she dances in a group, and she used to edit a magazine. She works in a cafe in Charing Cross now. She told us that she had seen another job that she would like to do. It was working in a care home for the elderly. If she were to get the job, it would mean that she would be helping with their teas and coffees and lunches. It also meant that she would be helping with the activities, such as bingo and singalongs. Lord Bertie and Charlie didn't even know what bingo was! Melanie told us that she had a boyfriend who had learning difficulties. She said that she would like to look after her Mum and Dad when they got old. But, every time she said that, her Dad joked, "Oh no! Please, God! No!"

Peter was a dancer. He was twenty six years old. He said that dancing was the love of his life. He had travelled the world. He had danced in Spain, Portugal and America. He told us that the two best moments of his life were doing a solo at Sadler's Wells and meeting the Queen. He told us that he also liked football. He said that he supported Arsenal, but his Dad supported Spurs.

Sean was twenty years old and he was a really good athlete. He won two silver medals in South Africa for swimming and he won a gold medal in the Special Olympics. He told us that he went to college where he made craft objects like Christmas decorations and necklaces that were sold on a stall as part of an enterprise scheme.

We all really enjoyed our time with the group. It was somehow reassuring and warm and funny. I asked Mr Burns if we could arrange a large donation to the group, and he said it was already done.

---- ✳ ✳ ✳ ----

Connie stayed at our house for most of the summer. Some of the chaps from school dropped by from time to time. And we did a bit of visiting, too. Mind you, it was a good job that we had such a big house just to fit Issy in. I had no idea that one small baby could turn such a huge house upside down!

The big event of the year was Aunty Ann and Uncle Charlie's wedding. They had a Spanish wedding planner, who hurried about the place taking small steps as though his legs were tied together with an elastic band. Every time somebody spoke to him, he had this habit of lowering his left arm a little and pushing his right hip out a bit and putting his right arm behind his back. Then he would flick his head back and say, "Senor? You wish to speak with me?" I think that maybe he thought that he was dancing the part of a bull fighter. Connie and I kept on calling him, just to see him do it. When Aunty Ann noticed what we were doing, she told us to stop it. But, then she started doing it herself! And then, when he wasn't there, she pretended to be him. She flounced around the room like a flamenco dancer saying, "I can make that gorgeth and I can make that gorgeth and I

can make that magnithico." We roared with laughter. Connie and I always laughed when Aunty Ann was around.

Aunty Ann decided that she was going to teach Uncle Charlie to do a dance. It was traditional for the bride and groom to do a waltz together to start the dancing at their wedding. But that wasn't Aunty Ann's style. She decided that she wanted to do a made up dance.

Uncle Charlie was an "anything to make you happy" kind of a chap, but I don't think that he had ever done anything quite like this before. Poor chap. We were in our TV lounge. It's quite a small room, with two settees and two chairs. That is pretty well all that's in it, but we probably use that room more than all of the other rooms put together. We were all in there. Lord Bertie in the corner, me and Connie, Mum and Dad, with Issy in a little carry cot in front of them. Aunty Ann and Uncle Charlie and Mr Burns in the other corner.

We pushed the furniture back and Aunty Ann put some music on, and then she dragged Uncle Charlie up to teach him the dance. The song that she had chosen to be the first song of their wedding reception was her favourite song of all time. It was called "See My Baby Jive" by a British singer called Roy Wood.

Aunty Ann got Uncle Charlie to stand behind her and take two steps forward and two steps back. He couldn't even do that properly. He was hopeless. Mum got up and Uncle Charlie sat down. Mum and Aunty Ann did the dance for us. They had been dancing it since they were teenagers. They made it look easy. Then they did it again with Aunty Ann on one side of Uncle Charlie and Mum on the other. He was still hopeless. He kept standing still at the wrong time and either Mum or Aunty Ann would bump into him. It was so funny to watch him trying so hard.

In the weeks leading up to the wedding, Mum gave Uncle Charlie secret dance lessons. I think he was frightened of letting Aunty

belle me, At Sour

Ann down on the big day. To be honest, I think that he would crawl over hot coals for her if he thought it would make her happy.

In the days before the wedding. Connie and I tried to make ourselves scarce. Manuel was flouncing about the house making everything "gorgeth, abtholutely gorgeth". Mum spent all of her time with Issy. Dad continued to run PNP. Lord Bertie took Connie and me down to the lake to teach us "the art of fly fishing".

George, Charlie's other brother came over a few days before the wedding. They took Dad down to London for a bachelor party. We were too young.

On the night before the wedding, Manuel arranged for the chef to prepare a beautiful meal. It was great. We sat around chatting and stayed up really late.

The wedding was really nice. It had a Spanish theme. All of the men were dressed like matadors (without the hats). Lord Bertie insisted on wearing his old trainers.

But he wouldn't be Lord Bertie if he looked like everybody else. Aunty Ann had a tight red dress like a flamenco dancer and the musicians played Spanish guitars.

Then Aunty Ann did the funniest thing. Dad was "giving her away". Mum was sitting with Issy. I was waiting to walk down the aisle. And Aunty Ann put her Cleveland Indians shirt on over her dress! She said it was her lucky shirt and she wanted to be married in it. If she hadn't stopped for a few seconds to swap her Birmingham City football club shirt for that shirt, it might have been her that was knocked down instead of that other woman. It might have been Aunty Ann who was seriously injured, or worse, she could have been killed.

Dad asked Aunty Ann if she was ready. She replied that she was born ready. When Aunty Ann walked down the aisle, everybody had broad smiles on their faces. Including Uncle Charlie. The only person who didn't smile was Manuel. He put the palms of his

134

hands to his face and his assistant fanned him with the hymn sheets.

It was a beautiful day. Aunty Ann held Issy on the wedding photographs. When they got up to dance at the reception, Uncle Charlie was absolutely hopeless. He was so bad that he gave up half way through. Everybody clapped anyway. Mum took his place. Aunty Ann and Mum danced in the middle of the dance floor and everybody stood around the side and clapped in time with the music.

My family and friends made me happier than any amount of money ever could. I looked round at everybody I loved and I realised that I had won the lottery long before I had ever bought a ticket. I had the best family in the world. That was worth more than anything money could ever buy.

Our new friends from the Acton Down's Syndrome Group got up to dance and then we all joined in. I held Issy in my arms and danced with her. I would always dance with her. Well, I'm a big brother now.

Other titles by E.R.Reilly

Harriet the Horrible

Best Friends

Rashnu

Tall Tales

Gnome Alone

One Boy, One Club, One Dream

The Amazing Time Travelling Adventures of Prof. McGinty
in Ancient Greece

Mirror Mirror

Contact us at

SANTIAGO PRESS

PO BOX 8808

BIRMINGHAM

B30 2LR

santiago@reilly19.freeserve.co.uk